IT'S MY STATE!

LOUISIANA

Ruth Bjorklund

Andy Steinitz

Marshall Cavendish
Benchmark

Other Marshall Cavendish Offices:
Marshall Cavendish International (Asia) Private Limited, 1 New Industrial Road, Singapore 536196 • Marshall Cavendish International (Thailand) Co Ltd. 253 Asoke, 12th Flr, Sukhumvit 21 Road, Klongtoey Nua, Wattana, Bangkok 10110, Thailand • Marshall Cavendish (Malaysia) Sdn Bhd, Times Subang, Lot 46, Subang Hi-Tech Industrial Park, Batu Tiga, 40000 Shah Alam, Selangor Darul Ehsan, Malaysia

Marshall Cavendish is a trademark of Times Publishing Limited

All websites were available and accurate when this book was sent to press.

Library of Congress Cataloging-in-Publication Data
Bjorklund, Ruth.
        Louisiana / Ruth Bjorklund, Andy Steinitz. — 2nd ed.
            p. cm. — (It's my state!)
        Includes index.
        ISBN 978-1-60870-051-6
        1. Louisiana—Juvenile literature. I. Steinitz, Andy. II. Title.
    F369.3.B58   2011
    976.3—dc22   2010003925

Second Edition developed for Marshall Cavendish Benchmark by RJF Publishing LLC (www.RJFpublishing.com)
Series Designer, Second Edition: Tammy West/Westgraphix LLC
Editor, Second Edition: Brian Fitzgerald

All maps, illustrations, and graphics © Marshall Cavendish Corporation. Maps and artwork on pages 6, 52, 53, 75, 76, and back cover by Christopher Santoro. Map and graphics on pages 9 and 42 by Westgraphix LLC.

The photographs in this book are used by permission and through the courtesy of:
Front cover: David Muench/Getty Images and Blaine Harrington III/Alamy (inset).
Alamy: Juniors Bildarchiv, 5; Goss Images, 12, 54; Jeff Greenberg, 13, 62; North Wind Picture Archives, 23; Jim West, 36; Mira, 38; David Seawell, 64; Brian Gauvin, 68; Art Directors & TRIP (top), 70; John Cancalosi, 74. **AP Images:** 61; Jim Hudelson, 55; Mike Dunlap, 59. **Getty Images:** Jodie Griggs, 4 (top); Diane Collins and Jordan Hollender, 4 (bottom); Tyrone Turner/National Geographic, 11; DEA/BELLANI, 15; Joe Sartore/National Geographic, 16; David Sanger (top) and Joel Simon (bottom), 18; Stephen Cooper, 19; MPI/Stringer, 24, 27, 29; Roger Viollet, 28; Apic/Hulton Archives, 32; Robert W. Kelley/Time & Life Pictures, 34; Paul J. Richards/AFP, 40; Dimitrios Kambouris/WireImage, 41; Don Craven/Time & Life Images, 44; Mario Tama, 45 (top), 46, 65; Astrid Stawiarz, 45 (bottom); Skip Bolen/WireImage, 47; Leon Morris/Redferns, 49; Andy Lyons, 72. **Library of Congress:** LC-USZ62-111070, 31. **Courtesy of the Louisiana Division of Archaeology:** Drawing by Jon Gibson, 22. **NASA:** NASA/Goddard Space Flight Center Scientific Visualization Studio, 17. **National Geographic Stock:** Annie Griffiths Belt, 8; James L. Stanfield, 20; Joel Sartore, 50–51. **Shutterstock:** Stephen Helstowski, 10; Gregory Pelt, 14; Caitlin Mirra, 35, 56; sarka, 70 (bottom); Hywit Dimyadi, 71; Louis Bourgeois, 73.

Printed in Malaysia (T).
135642

CONTENTS

State Flower: Magnolia

Magnolia trees can be found in swamps, lowland forests, and coastal plains. Some reach a height of 100 feet (30 meters). Flowers bloom in early summer in a number of colors, from white to purple to yellow.

State Bird: Brown Pelican

Brown pelicans nest on coastal islands and along the shore of the Gulf of Mexico. Brown pelicans were once so abundant in Louisiana that its nickname is the Pelican State. But brown pelicans nearly became extinct, or died out, in the 1950s. The birds were eating a pesticide called DDT, which made their eggs break easily. DDT was banned in 1972, and conservationists have since helped restore the brown pelican population.

State Tree: Bald Cypress

The bald cypress is a conifer, a type of tree that usually keeps its needlelike leaves year-round. But the bald cypress sheds its needles in winter, which is how the tree got its name. Bald cypresses grow in warm coastal areas and swamps. They can live for several hundred years.

State Mammal: Louisiana Black Bear

Louisiana black bears weigh up to 400 pounds (180 kilograms). They are shy creatures, making their homes in hollow logs, briar patches, and brush piles. By 1992, the population of Louisiana black bears had shrunk so low that the animals were declared threatened. Today, only four hundred to five hundred bears are left. Louisianans are working to prevent their state mammal from dying out.

State Crustacean: Crawfish

In 1983, Louisiana became the first state to select an official state crustacean. Crawfish are small freshwater cousins to the sea-dwelling lobster. Found in marshes, rivers, lakes, ponds, and swamps throughout the state, crawfish have been a flavorful and important source of food for centuries. Other names for the creature are crayfish, crawdad, and mudbug.

State Dog: Catahoula Leopard Dog

The Catahoula leopard dog is a breed that probably developed in the 1500s when residents of the region bred dogs raised by American Indians with dogs brought from Spain. The Catahoula leopard dog has shiny eyes, a spotted coat, and webbed feet that are useful for swimming. Most of these dogs are good hunters and trackers. Many are trained to herd livestock, such as pigs, on farms and ranches.

The Pelican State

Lush, watery Louisiana seems forever in bloom. Billions of gallons of river water wash through the state and spill out into the Gulf of Mexico. Boundless streams, bayous (marshy creeks), lakes, ponds, swamps, and marshlands bathe the land and give life to a rich variety of vegetation and wildlife.

Prairies to the Sea

The state of Louisiana is a boot-shaped area of land covering about 43,560 square miles (112,820 square kilometers). More than 8,200 square miles (21,200 sq km) are underwater. The state is divided into sixty-four parishes. These divisions are known as counties in most other states. The state capital, Baton Rouge, is in East Baton Rouge Parish. New Orleans, the largest city in Louisiana, is in Orleans Parish, in the southeastern part of the state.

One of the nation's most important rivers, the Mississippi River, winds and curves through the state. The Mississippi empties into the Gulf of Mexico, as do other rivers in Louisiana, such as the Atchafalaya, Ouachita, Sabine, Pearl, and Red rivers. Many areas of Louisiana are low-lying wetlands, swamps, and marshes. However, the state also has rolling hills,

Quick Facts

LOUISIANA BORDERS

North	Arkansas
South	Gulf of Mexico
East	Mississippi
West	Texas

Waves hit the Chandeleur Islands, a chain of barrier islands off the southeastern coast of Louisiana.

forests, and grass prairies. The highest point in the state, Driskill Mountain, is located in northwestern Louisiana and rises 535 feet (163 m). The lowest points are near the coast, where the land dips below sea level. Just off the coast, many islands protect the delicate inner shore. These islands are called barrier islands.

The Gulf Coastal Plain

The entire state of Louisiana is part of a natural geographic region called the Gulf Coastal Plain. The Tunica Hills lie in a group of parishes known as the Florida Parishes in the eastern part of the state. Covered with flowering trees such as magnolia, sweetgum, dogwood, and hydrangea, the Tunica Hills also feature forests of beech, oak, and other hardwoods. Nearby West Feliciana Parish contains the wetlands and woodlands where the great naturalist John Audubon studied and painted wildlife for his famous book *Birds of America*. While exploring the region, Audubon painted more than eighty birds, including the hooded merganser, pigeon hawk, white pelican, and blue heron, as well as the now-extinct passenger pigeon.

Louisiana Parishes

Louisiana has 64 parishes.

Spanish moss hangs from trees in the Louisiana bayou. It is easy to see why American Indians called the moss tree hair.

The Pearl River forms the state's southeastern border with Mississippi. The Pearl River splits into many channels and small, marshy, slow-moving waterways called bayous. These bayous and channels form large swamps and marshlands where trees are draped with Spanish moss. Honey Island Swamp, near Slidell, is the largest in the area. There, bald eagles, alligators, egrets, and wild turkeys roam among the oaks, cypress, and water lilies. More than 50 square miles (130 sq km) of pristine wetland is filled with wild creatures and plants.

The Mississippi Floodplain is an area of fertile land that lies along the banks of the famous river that winds through the state. The major cities of New Orleans and Baton Rouge are found in the Floodplain. Over time, the river has reshaped

Rainwater carved grooves into this reconstructed levee in New Orleans.

the surrounding landscape. Levees, or ridges 10 to 15 feet (3 to 5 m) high, stop the river from flooding nearby areas. Some levees have formed naturally as sediment—rocks, dirt, sand, and other material—is pushed up onto land by the river as it flows or floods. People also build levees or strengthen natural levees with sediment or concrete. Beyond the levee walls, the land is very flat and filled with ponds, swamps, and bayous. Slight changes in ground level cause these areas to collect rain and floodwater.

The southern end of the Mississippi River opens into a delta. The river delta is a system of slow-moving channels of water and rich, muddy soil. There, the Mississippi drops about 500 million

Quick Facts

GREAT TOWER OF SALT

Avery Island rises 152 feet (46 m) above sea level in the marshes near the central Louisiana coast. The island is actually the peak of a towering dome of salt. It is one of five salt domes in the area. Centuries ago, a layer of salt deep underground pushed through Earth's surface to form these salty structures.

A young explorer paddles a boat down the Atchafalaya River in southern Louisiana.

tons (453 million metric tons) of soil every year. When the mud blocks a channel, the water pushes through to form a new route.

The entire coast west of the delta into Texas is an estuary, where the freshwater of the Mississippi River and its offshoots meets the salty water of the Gulf of Mexico. The largest wilderness swamp in the nation, the Atchafalaya Basin, was created by all this water. Hundreds of species of birds stop there during their migrations. Fish fill its swamps, and reptiles and amphibians live among its tall cordgrass. The swamps are also home to threatened and endangered species, such as the Louisiana black bear, pallid sturgeon, and American alligator.

The southwestern part of the state has many remarkable landforms, such as barrier islands, marshes, grasslands, beaches, and cheniers—oak-tree-covered islands formed from crushed shells and sand. Rare and endangered creatures, such as the piping plover and the Kemp's Ridley sea turtle, find refuge along these coastal areas. Herons, egrets, pelicans, eagles, and a host of other shorebirds are also found along the Louisiana coast. Going north, a traveler will pass through the Cajun Prairie, where once-treeless grasslands have been replaced by thousands of acres of rice fields and pastures. This farmland gives way to rolling hills dotted with pine trees. These hills stretch toward the northwest border of the state.

Climate and Seasons

Louisiana's warm temperatures and steady rains make the state a year-round paradise for gardeners. But Louisianans must also deal with tornadoes, hurricanes, other wind and rain storms, and often extremely high humidity (the amount of moisture in the air).

Summers in Louisiana are long and hot. Winters are short and mild. In the northern city of Shreveport, the temperature typically stays above 90 degrees Fahrenheit (32 degrees Celsius) for most of the summer. The high humidity makes northern Louisiana steamy and uncomfortable in summer. During northern Louisiana's coolest month, January, temperatures are about

On a hot summer day, children cool off in a fountain in St. Tammany Parish in southeastern Louisiana.

46 °F (8 °C). Record-setting temperatures in the state have occurred in the north. On August 10, 1936, the temperature in Plain Dealing reached 114 °F (46 °C). Minden recorded the coldest temperature, −16 °F (−27 °C), back in February 1899.

The Gulf of Mexico creates a steadier climate for southern Louisiana. The gulf affects the winds and the air temperature, resulting in fewer extremes of hot and cold. Breezes from the gulf cool off the land in summer and warm it in winter. Summer temperatures in southern Louisiana average 84 °F (29 °C). The winter temperatures average about 55 °F (13 °C).

Wind and rain affect the entire state. Northern Louisiana is in the path of strong winds that blow across the Great Plains and is on the southern edge of a region known as "Tornado Alley." Spring is the most threatening time of year for thunderstorms, hailstorms, and tornadoes, as cold air from the Great Plains runs into warm air from the Gulf of Mexico. When the weather fronts

Hurricane Katrina brought winds of more than 145 miles (233 km) per hour when it struck Louisiana.

collide, air begins to swirl and forms funnel clouds and hail. Summer brings unstable weather to southern Louisiana. Violent hurricanes batter the coast with raging winds, high surf, flooding, and heavy rain. The worst hurricane to hit the state was Hurricane Katrina, which struck in August 2005.

In Louisiana, precipitation is usually in the form of rain. Yearly rainfall in Louisiana averages from 51 inches (130 centimeters) in the northwest to 66 inches (168 cm) in the southeast. Snow occasionally falls in the north. In winter, frost forms when polar air moves down from Alaska and Canada and settles over the state. From late fall to early spring, farmers must protect their crops from the effects of frost. The growing season is measured by the number of days between the last spring frost and the first fall frost. Farmers statewide enjoy very long growing seasons.

Louisiana Wildlife

As naturalist John Audubon noted, the variety of Louisiana's wildlife seems endless. Many types of trees, shrubs, and grasses thrive in the fields and marshes and along the coast. Wildflowers and other blooms fill the fields in the spring and summer. Deer, black bears, and red wolves live in the pine-filled woods, while catfish, bass, trout, crawfish, and alligators swim in the swamps and rivers. The state's coastal marshes, islands, and beaches are home to brown pelicans, nutria (a type of rodent), crappies (a type of fish), redear sunfish, and green tree frogs. An abundance of sea life, including oysters, rays, sharks,

Nutrias look like beavers with tails like those of big, fat rats. They feast on the plants in Louisiana's wetlands, which is causing the soil to erode, or wear away.

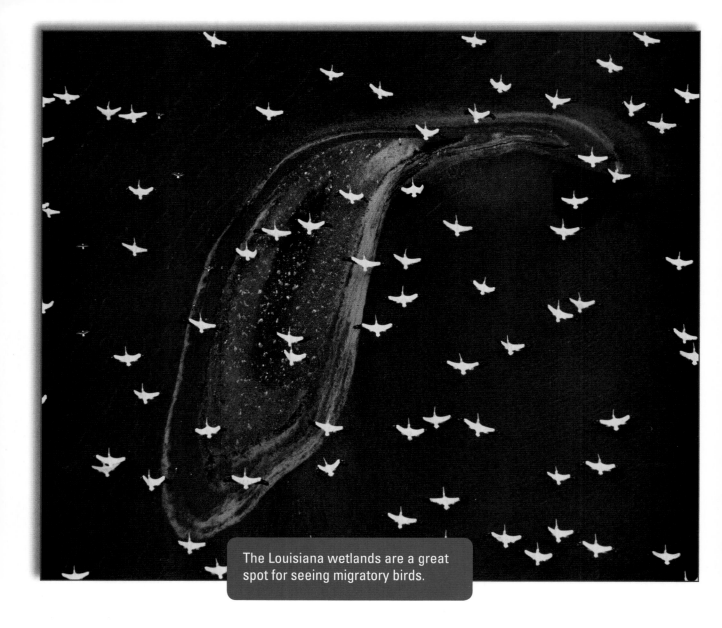

The Louisiana wetlands are a great spot for seeing migratory birds.

speckled trout, and bluefish, lives just offshore in the Gulf. Huge numbers of crabs and shrimp inhabit local waters, too. While many plants and animals can be found in abundance, concerned citizens throughout the state are acting to protect Louisiana's rare or endangered species. These include sea turtles, the Louisiana quillwort (a grasslike water plant), and birds such as the red-cockaded woodpecker, least tern, and piping plover.

Louisiana's life-giving rivers can also cause serious problems. Every summer, an area that scientists call a "dead zone" forms off the coast of Louisiana. As the

Mississippi River flows past farms, it carries away some of the fertilizers that have been used on the farmland. When the river empties into the Gulf of Mexico, the fertilizers are deposited along the coast, contributing to a burst of algae growth. This causes a loss of oxygen in the water, and the low oxygen levels kill fish, shrimp, crabs, and other sea life. In recent summers, the size of the dead zone has been close to 8,000 square miles (20,700 sq km)—about the size of New Jersey. To try to fix the problem, people all along the Mississippi River are learning ways to keep fertilizers out of the water. They are building barriers and filters that help prevent fertilizers from spreading into rivers.

This satellite image shows the Gulf of Mexico dead zone off the coast of Louisiana.

Plants & Animals

American Alligator

The American alligator is the largest reptile in North America. The species has existed for 200 million years. Alligators live in Louisiana's rivers, lakes, canals, and bayous. On average, they are 13 feet (4 m) long and weigh 450 to 600 pounds (200 to 270 kg). Alligators eat just about anything, but they mostly dine on fish, turtles, snails, and small mammals. American alligators were endangered in the 1950s but have since made a comeback.

Spanish Moss

Unlike other types of moss, Spanish moss grows only on trees, and not on fences, buildings, or telephone poles. It is not actually a moss, however. It is an epiphyte, which means it grows on other plants for support. It does not harm or feed on the tree on which it lives. Fragrant, tiny flowers burst forth from the moss in spring.

Western Cottonmouth Snake

This dark-colored snake lives near water and is a very poisonous member of the pit viper family. While waiting to attack small animals, a cottonmouth lies coiled with its head flung back and its cotton-colored mouth wide open. Once it spies its prey (the animal it is going to eat), the snake strikes quickly and snaps shut its powerful jaws. Some people call these snakes trapjaw snakes or water moccasins.

Snowy Egret

Snowy egrets live year-round in Louisiana, nesting near swamps. The bird is 20 to 40 inches (50 to 100 cm) tall, with long black legs, yellow toes, a black bill, and white feathers. During the mating season, a snowy egret will grow a wispy plume of long, white feathers. In the late 1800s, it was stylish for women to wear hats with feathers. Plume hunters nearly wiped out the snowy egret population until laws were passed to protect the birds.

Catfish

There are several species of catfish. Many, such as the blue, flathead, channel, and hardhead catfish, are found in some of Louisiana's freshwater lakes, ponds, and rivers. The blue catfish is the largest in North America. It can weigh more than 100 pounds (45 kg).

Live Oak

Live oaks are large, spreading evergreen trees. Live oaks got their name because they grow new leaves as soon as the old ones die. Reaching heights of 40 to 50 feet (12 to 15 m), live oaks are often draped in Spanish moss. The wood is very dense and was once used for shipbuilding. Many animals, such as wild turkeys, foxes, rabbits, and black bears, rely on the acorns of live oaks for food.

From the Beginning

Louisiana's past is as complex and shifting as the Mississippi River flowing across its land. From ancient American Indian artists to Caribbean pirates, from French-Acadian refugees to African-American jazz musicians, Louisiana is a state with a people and history like no other.

The First People

Prehistoric groups of people first arrived in present-day Louisiana during the last ice age, about 10,000 BCE. It was a much cooler and drier place then. These people were nomadic hunters, meaning they followed their food from place to place. As early as 3400 BCE, some built extraordinary mounds of earth. In northern Louisiana, in an area called Watson Brake, scientists have discovered eleven huge mounds that rise up to 25 feet (8 m). Scientists are still puzzled by the purpose of the mounds.

In addition to hunting, the prehistoric people fished in the rivers and gathered fruits and nuts. Scientists refer to these tribes as the Mound Builders. In later years, the descendants of Mound Builders used tools, worked metal, and decorated pottery. Some began to stay in one place year-round. They traded with tribes as far away as present-day Wisconsin.

The people who met the European explorers in the sixteenth century were descendants of the Mound Builders. These American Indians lived along the

A jazz band plays at Preservation Hall in New Orleans. Music is a big part of the city's rich history.

This illustration shows the complex layout of the earthen mounds and terraces at Poverty Point in northern Louisiana. The mounds were built by American Indians more than three thousand years ago.

coast and waterways of southeastern Louisiana. Most were farmers who tended crops of maize, melons, squash, beans, and millet—a type of grain. Men hunted bear, rabbit, deer, and wild turkeys with bows and arrows. But the major sources of food for southern groups were fish, clams, and oysters.

Their villages were groups of homes made from poles and thatched leaves. For transportation, the American Indians built dugout canoes from trees. People wore dyed and painted clothing made from animal skins. Both men and women wore jewelry—anklets, earrings, necklaces, and nose rings. Men and women also wore tattoos that symbolized their achievements in life.

Many different American Indian tribes lived across Louisiana. Most belonged to one of six major cultural groups. The Tunica and Natchez culture groups were found in the northeast. People who spoke the Muskogean language lived in the central regions. These included the Natchez, Houma, and Choctaw tribes. The Caddo, including the Natchitoches, lived in the northwest. The Chitimacha and Attakapa peoples lived along the coast and swamps of the southwest.

European Encounters

In 1519, a Spanish explorer, Alvarez de Pineda, traveled through the region and reported seeing a river flowing with gold. What he probably saw was the Mississippi River. Another Spanish explorer, Hernando de Soto, undoubtedly explored the Mississippi in 1541. DeSoto led an expedition for gold through much of America's southeast. However, he died before his army entered Louisiana. The Europeans brought diseases that quickly spread among the American Indian population. Many died before the next major contact with European explorers.

In 1682, French explorer René-Robert Cavelier, sieur de La Salle, traveled down the Mississippi River. He claimed the area that now includes Louisiana and some of the neighboring states for the French king, Louis XIV. La Salle named the territory Louisiane in honor of the king.

After La Salle's claim, Pierre and Jean-Baptiste Le Moyne set sail from France and founded an outpost near present-day Biloxi, Mississippi, in 1699. The settlers encountered American Indians and built forts to protect themselves from the Spanish, who had settled in present-day Florida and Mexico, and the British, who had established colonies along the continent's east coast.

Meanwhile in Europe, France, Spain, and their allies were at war with Great Britain and its allies. France needed money to support the war effort. Louisiana was not a moneymaking colony for France, so the French government decided to turn it over

Quick Facts

THE FOUNDER OF NEW ORLEANS

Jean-Baptiste Le Moyne was eighteen when he helped his brother settle the first colony in the Louisiana Territory. Two years later, he was appointed governor of the territory. In the 1720s, he helped pick the site for New Orleans and named it for Philippe II, Duke of Orleans, who in effect ruled France at the time (because the king was still a child). The city became the capital of the territory in 1723.

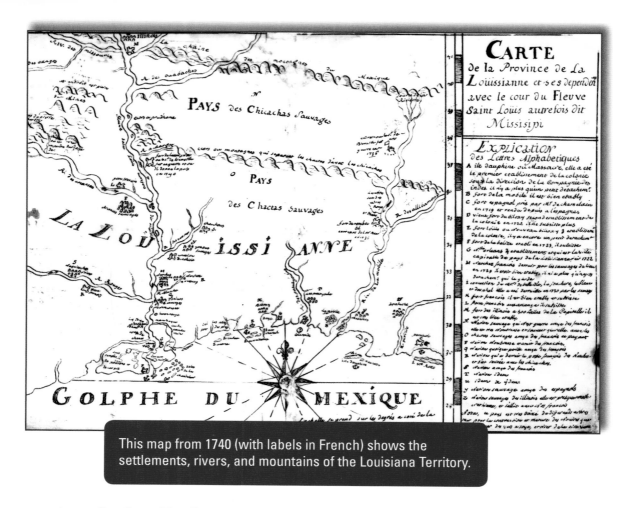

This map from 1740 (with labels in French) shows the settlements, rivers, and mountains of the Louisiana Territory.

to private funders. The first permanent settlement was founded in 1714 at present-day Natchitoches. From 1717 to 1731, a Scottish economist named John Law convinced thousands of people to come to Louisiana. Investors in France funded the settlements. Some settlers were prisoners shipped out of France by government officials who did not want these criminals in France. Others were Europeans who were promised land and livestock in exchange for settlement. So many Germans accepted Law's offer that the Mississippi shoreline west of New Orleans became known as the German Coast. Law promised riches, but the pioneers found the land to be an insect-filled swamp full of deadly tropical diseases and a native population unhappy about the newcomers' arrival.

More than five thousand slaves from West Africa and the French-owned Caribbean islands arrived during that period, too. In addition to working against their will, the slaves suffered from the intense heat, insects, and disease. But they brought valuable farming knowledge to the land. Tobacco and indigo became cash crops. Yet farming settlements did not make anyone wealthy. The investors stopped paying, and Law's company eventually went bankrupt.

Meanwhile, the Spanish built Fort Los Adaes in northwestern Louisiana. It became the capital of Texas Province in 1729. As European settlements grew and prospered, the colonists took over more and more of the land belonging to the native people. Many tribes had to fend for themselves or pick a European nation to befriend. Both the Natchez and the Chickasaw groups fought the French. However, the Choctaw stood by the French in many conflicts.

In the mid–1750s, most European powers, including France, were again at war. In North America, the war between France and Great Britain was called the French and Indian War. Many battles were fought on North American soil. By 1762, the French sensed defeat. They did not want to lose their territory to the British. Instead, France gave all its land west of the Mississippi River, plus New Orleans, to its ally Spain. When the war ended in 1763, France surrendered the remainder of its North American territory to Great Britain.

By that time, the first of thousands of French colonists had begun to arrive from Canada. The Acadians had lived on the island of Nova Scotia in eastern Canada for more than a century. In 1755, the British demanded that the Acadians sign a loyalty oath to Great Britain. When the Acadians refused, the British forced them out. Many Acadians traveled thousands of miles to reach the former French colony of Louisiana. There, the Acadian refugees later became known as Cajuns.

American Revolution

In 1775, the thirteen British colonies along the east coast of America began their fight for independence from Great Britain. The Spanish governor of Louisiana helped the colonists. He allowed goods to travel by boat up the Mississippi River to supply the American revolutionaries. In 1783, the colonies won their independence and became the United States of America. Through a deal with Spain, New Orleans became an important port city for the newly independent nation.

In 1800, Spain signed a treaty that gave the huge Louisiana Territory back to France. The area included all or part of fourteen future U.S. states, not just Louisiana. U.S. president Thomas Jefferson worried that France would close New Orleans to American shipping. The United States offered to buy the territory. At the time, French emperor Napoleon Bonaparte was leading a military campaign through Europe. In 1803, to raise money, he sold the entire Louisiana Territory for $15 million. This sale, known as the Louisiana Purchase, greatly increased the size of the United States. To make governing the region easier, the territory was divided. One part was called the Territory of Orleans. This area included most of present-day Louisiana.

Pirates and Generals

By 1810, the future state's population grew to more than 76,000 people. New steam-powered ships began traveling the Mississippi River, carrying tons of goods and supplies to and from the expanding nation. New Orleans became the seventh-largest city in the United States. On April 30, 1812, Louisiana became the eighteenth state.

In the early 1800s, pirates were operating in the Caribbean Sea. Many brought stolen goods to New Orleans to sell. Some pirates, known as privateers, were given permission by the United States to attack any non-American ship. The British began fighting the privateers, but they also started kidnapping American sailors and invading American waters. In response, the United States declared war on Great Britain in 1812.

During the War of 1812, British generals saw the importance of New Orleans as a seaport and planned an attack. They invited one of the most notorious pirates, Jean Lafitte, to join their navy. But Louisiana's governor ordered a raid on Lafitte's harbor at Barataria Bay and captured his brother Pierre. Meanwhile, American general Andrew Jackson prepared to defend the city with whoever was willing to fight, including free blacks and Choctaw warriors. Jean Lafitte gathered other pirates to help Jackson's troops in return for Pierre's freedom. On January 8, 1815, General Jackson's motley army defeated a British force that was

This illustration shows General Andrew Jackson's army, including black soldiers, fighting during the Battle of New Orleans in January 1815.

twice its size. What came to be known as the Battle of New Orleans was a great victory. Little did the opposing armies know that two weeks earlier the United States and Great Britain had signed a treaty that ended the war. Andrew Jackson became a national hero and was elected president of the United States in 1828.

A Growing Economy

Large Louisiana farms, or plantations, became very profitable in the first half of the nineteenth century. Cotton grew well in the northern part of the state, and sugar thrived in the south. White landowners operated the plantations and used black slaves to perform the hard labor of planting and harvesting crops. Some white landowners grew wealthy as a result of slave labor and the ease with which they could ship their crops up and down the Mississippi River. One of these

This photo from the 1800s shows Oak Alley, a famous plantation along the Mississippi River. Today, visitors can explore Oak Alley to learn about what plantation life was like in the pre–Civil War era.

people was Zachary Taylor. He made Baton Rouge his adopted home before being elected U.S. president in 1848. A year later, the city became the capital of Louisiana.

New Orleans thrived as the second-busiest port in the United States. From 1820 to 1860, hundreds of thousands of immigrants arrived from Europe, South America, and the Caribbean. The city had more free blacks than any other city in the United States. Life became a mix of many different cultures. In 1843, the University of Louisiana (later renamed Tulane University) was founded in the city.

The War Between the States

Slavery was a major topic of debate in the United States in the first half of the nineteenth century. Most people living in Northern states wanted to abolish, or end, slavery. But Southern states relied on slavery to support their economy.

In 1860, Abraham Lincoln, an antislavery politician, was elected president. South Carolina decided to secede, or withdraw, from the United States (the Union). Louisiana was one of ten more Southern states that, in 1861, also seceded. These states formed the Confederate States of America. Lincoln refused to accept the withdrawal of these Southern states from the Union.

In April 1861, Confederate soldiers fired on and captured Fort Sumter in South Carolina. It was the start of the Civil War, which would continue for four years.

Few battles took place within Louisiana. Early in the war, Union troops occupied New Orleans and Baton Rouge, taking control of the ports and most of the lower Mississippi River boat traffic. The Union army declared New Orleans the capital of all the Union-controlled land in Louisiana. Louisiana's Confederate government moved its capital from Baton Rouge to Shreveport. Thousands of escaped slaves joined the Union army. Many were organized into regiments to defend New Orleans and other key cities. The Confederacy eventually lost the war. In April 1865, Confederate general Robert E. Lee surrendered to Union general Ulysses S. Grant. Later that year, Louisiana was one of thirty states that approved the Thirteenth Amendment to the U.S. Constitution, which abolished slavery in the United States.

African-American Union soldiers fought bravely during the Battle of Fort Hudson, Louisiana, in May 1863.

The Reconstruction Era and Beyond

Louisiana was a different place after the Civil War. Crops and farms were ruined, homes were destroyed, schools were empty, roads were unusable, and banks and other businesses failed. Angry at the loss of their old way of life, many Southerners resented Northerners who came to the South. They called them "carpetbaggers," because their traveling bags were made from carpets.

Though slaves were now free, Louisiana and other Southern states passed new laws known as Black Codes. These codes took away many of the rights promised to African Americans, such as the freedom to have certain jobs or live in certain places. In July 1866, a group of politicians met in New Orleans to discuss issues including voting rights. A crowd of white people, including police officers, killed more than thirty black people and several of their white supporters.

This incident and other events led the U.S. Congress to pass the first of several laws called the Reconstruction Acts. The acts put the former Confederate states under U.S. Army control. Like the other states, Louisiana could not return to the Union as a state without drafting and accepting a new state constitution. Louisiana citizens adopted a new constitution that gave some rights to members of all races and voting rights to black men. The constitution also called for at least one public school in every parish. All children ages six to eighteen could attend, no matter the color of their skin. On June 25, 1868, Louisiana was officially readmitted as a state.

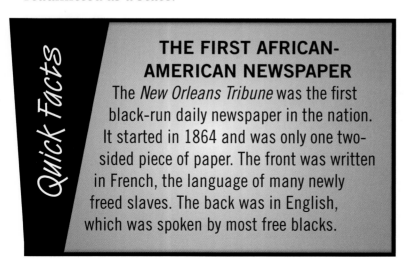

Quick Facts

THE FIRST AFRICAN-AMERICAN NEWSPAPER

The *New Orleans Tribune* was the first black-run daily newspaper in the nation. It started in 1864 and was only one two-sided piece of paper. The front was written in French, the language of many newly freed slaves. The back was in English, which was spoken by most free blacks.

Louisiana during this time was full of bold steps forward and violent reactions. John W. Menard was the first African American elected to Congress. But the election results were disputed, and he was never seated. In 1872,

THE RIOT IN NEW ORLEANS—THE FREEDMEN'S PROCESSION MARCHING TO THE INSTITUTE—THE STRUGGLE FOR THE FLAG.
[SKETCHED BY THEODORE R. DAVIS.]

THE RIOT IN NEW ORLEANS—SIEGE AND ASSAULT OF THE CONVENTION BY THE POLICE AND CITIZENS.—SKETCHED BY THEODORE R. DAVIS.
[SEE PAGE 355.]

P. B. S. Pinchback briefly served as governor, the first African American to hold that office. Some white Louisianans fought such changes with intimidation and violence. They created organizations such as the White League and the Ku Klux Klan. These groups terrorized African Americans and the whites who supported equal opportunities for African Americans.

In 1877, federal control of Reconstruction ended in Louisiana. The army left and new politicians came into power. They did very little to help Louisianans because they believed that was not the government's role. Much of the progress made during Reconstruction was stopped.

Life in the countryside remained difficult. Many people found jobs mining sulfur or salt or harvesting pine and cypress for lumber. More than sixty towns grew around lumber companies in Louisiana. Other towns grew along the newly built railroads that ran through the delta. Farmers from the Northeast and Midwest produced an abundance of rice in the prairies of southwest Louisiana.

However, many more landowners could not afford to run their plantations now that slaves no longer provided free labor. The solution was a system called

By the late 1800s, steam excavators were used in the exhausting work of sulfur mining.

sharecropping. Black and white farm laborers worked a portion of the land and gave a percentage of their earnings to the landowner. Usually money did not exchange hands. Instead, landowners would provide the sharecroppers with tools, food, and supplies on credit during the planting and growing seasons. When it was time to split the earnings after crops were harvested, most of the sharecroppers' portion went to the landowner to pay off the loans. Many former slaves found themselves working the same land and living in the same houses as they had before they were free.

By the end of the nineteenth century, nearly all the rights granted to African-American citizens in Louisiana had been taken away. White politicians who controlled the government passed many "Jim Crow" laws. These laws called for separation of the races in schools, in public places, and in public transportation. In 1892, a group of black leaders in New Orleans decided to challenge the laws. Homer Plessy, a shoemaker of black descent, boarded a whites-only train car and was arrested. The case went all the way to the U.S. Supreme Court. The Court ruled that segregation laws were legal as long as they provided for "equal" service to blacks and whites. The decision was a major blow to African Americans in their struggle for equal rights.

In 1898, a new state constitution required that black men must own property, be able to read and write, and pay a fee (called a poll tax) before they could vote. However, white men did not need to meet these requirements to vote. (At the time, no women were allowed to vote.) It would be many years before black Louisianans were given equal rights.

The 1900s

The new century brought a new industry—petroleum. After oil was found near Jennings in 1901, oil wells sprang up across the southern part of the state and later in the northwest near Shreveport and Bossier City. Pipelines were built to send oil from fields in Texas and Oklahoma to the port at Baton Rouge.

In 1927, heavy rains caused weeks of flooding along the banks of the Mississippi River between Missouri and the Gulf of Mexico. In Louisiana, the water broke through the levees that landowners had built in the lowlands. The river rose nearly 50 feet (15 m) at Baton Rouge. Hundreds of thousands of people were left homeless, and millions of dollars' worth of property was destroyed.

In 1928, Huey P. Long was elected governor of Louisiana. A year later, the United States entered a period of severe economic hardship known as the Great Depression. Millions of Americans were out of work. Long created jobs for Louisiana farmers who could not find employment elsewhere. They worked on large public improvement projects, such as roads, schools, and flood-control programs. Long taxed wealthy citizens and large

In Their Own Words

Every man to eat when there is something to eat; all to wear something when there is something to wear. . . . We had these great incomes in this country but the farmer, who plowed from sun up to sundown, who labored here from sun up to sundown for six days a week, wound up at the end of the day with practically nothing.

—Huey Long,
in a 1934 radio address

corporations and used the money to run social programs, such as providing free textbooks to public school students.

When the United States entered World War II in 1941, Louisiana farmers and factory workers provided much-needed supplies. The state was rich with oil and minerals that were important to the war effort. For the first time in the state's history, there were more citizens working in the cities than in rural areas. Baton Rouge nearly quadrupled in size. While men were fighting overseas, women worked in factories and in other jobs that used to be off-limits to them. The shipyards in New Orleans built many vessels for use in the war. After the war, the boom times in the cities continued. New tax laws invited more and more industry to the state.

Under Louisiana law, classrooms like this one in New Orleans were segregated until the 1950s.

Circumstances also started to improve for African Americans. The U.S. Supreme Court ruled in 1954 on a case that started in Kansas, called *Brown v. Board of Education of Topeka*. The Court overturned the earlier decision in Homer Plessy's case and said that it was not possible to have separate but equal schools for black children and white children. All schools had to be open to children of all races. Although the 1954 decision applied only to schools, it was an important legal step toward ending many other types of segregation—for example, on buses and trains, and in restaurants and other public places. Change did not come right away. But the 1954 decision gave hope to black citizens, who would see many of their civil rights restored over the next decades.

A Century Closes

Louisiana enjoyed decades of prosperity after World War II. Oil provided a lot of money and jobs for the state. But in the 1980s, oil prices declined around the world, and Louisiana went into another depression. To try to regain lost income, the state looked to its unique heritage. The government promoted tourism in the state. It also changed its gambling laws to allow riverboat casinos to open near New Orleans, Baton Rouge, Lake Charles, and Shreveport. From 1994 to 1999, tourism grew more in Louisiana than in any other state.

Billions of dollars in increased income earned from tourism and gambling helped the state in many ways. One area was the improvement of the public school system. In the late 1990s, Louisiana began repairing or replacing aged school buildings and raised teachers' salaries.

Hurricane Katrina and Recovery

Tragedy struck on August 29, 2005, when Hurricane Katrina raged over southeast Louisiana. Rain and strong winds created huge ocean waves that pounded New Orleans. Water levels

A view from the sky shows some of the widespread flooding in New Orleans after Hurricane Katrina.

A volunteer helps rebuild a New Orleans home that was destroyed by Hurricane Katrina.

rose in Lake Pontchartrain, just north of New Orleans, pouring water over the city's levees. Eventually some levees broke. Four-fifths of New Orleans was flooded. The southeast section called the Lower Ninth Ward and nearby St. Bernard Parish were almost entirely underwater.

About 1,500 people died. Around 900,000 lost their homes. Thousands flocked to shelters set up in the Superdome, the city's convention center, and other places, where they waited for days for any kind of assistance. Clean drinking water and food were hard to find. The government was slow to provide relief. After help arrived, some people settled in nearby cities, but a quarter of New Orleanians left for Texas and other neighboring states. Many people never came back.

Cleanup required a lot of hard work. The leftover debris could have filled the Superdome thirteen times. People from across the nation and the world came to help Louisiana, and residents began rebuilding levees, schools, other public buildings, and homes. In a matter of years, New Orleans became one of America's fastest-growing cities. Still, that was growth from a very low starting point, and it may be many years before the city of New Orleans returns to its pre-Katrina population.

Quick Facts

LENDING A HAND
In the years after Hurricane Katrina, many organizations and celebrities lent a hand. Musician Branford Marsalis and singer Harry Connick Jr. helped build a "village" of brightly painted homes for up-and-coming musicians. In the Lower Ninth Ward, actor Brad Pitt and the Make It Right Foundation helped build hurricane-proof houses that are also environmentally friendly.

Important Dates

★ **3400 BCE** Early inhabitants of modern-day Louisiana, the Mound Builders, make large hills at Watson Brake.

★ **1682** René-Robert Cavelier, sieur de La Salle, explores the Mississippi River and claims a huge area of land for King Louis XIV of France.

★ **1714** A French fort and trading center is established at modern-day Natchitoches, the first permanent settlement in the Louisiana Territory.

★ **1762** King Louis XV of France gives the large Louisiana Territory to his cousin, King Charles III of Spain.

★ **1800** Spain returns the Louisiana Territory to France.

★ **1803** France sells the Louisiana Territory to the United States.

★ **1812** Louisiana becomes a U.S. state on April 30.

★ **1815** The Battle of New Orleans, the last major battle of the War of 1812, is fought.

★ **1861** Louisiana secedes from the United States and joins the Confederacy.

★ **1865** The Confederacy loses the Civil War.

★ **1868** Louisiana is officially readmitted to the United States as a state.

★ **1901** Oil is discovered near Jennings.

★ **1927** Flooding along the Mississippi River causes widespread damage throughout the state.

★ **1928** Huey P. Long is elected governor and later helps create jobs during the Great Depression.

★ **1993** The first gambling casino in Louisiana opens in New Orleans.

★ **2003** Louisianans elect their first female governor, Kathleen Babineaux Blanco.

★ **2005** Hurricanes Katrina and Rita devastate southern Louisiana.

★ **2007** Bobby Jindal is elected governor of Louisiana. He becomes the first Indian-American governor in U.S. history.

★ **2010** The New Orleans Saints win their first Super Bowl.

The People

Ever since French colonists settled alongside native tribes, Louisiana has been a land of many traditions. The American Indians taught the European settlers many secrets to survival. These included which vegetables to grow, how to cook with native herbs and spices, where to fish and trap, and how to navigate the winding waterways by canoe. By the early eighteenth century, however, life was different. European diseases and violence between the tribes and colonists destroyed much of the American Indian population. The American Indians who survived moved to remote communities in the region or west to new territories. Today in Louisiana, there are only four small Indian reservations that are recognized by the federal government.

However, American Indian influence can be seen in hundreds of place names, such as *Atchafalaya*, *Natchitoches*, and *Kisatchie*. The word *bayou* comes

Quick Facts

THE RED STICK BOUNDARY

The name *Baton Rouge* is French for "red stick." The term comes from a custom of the Houma and Bayogoula American Indian groups. They used to dye a pole with animal blood and stake it in the ground to mark the boundary between their hunting grounds. The French called the bloody pole *le baton rouge.*

Three young Louisianans join in the fun during the world-famous Mardi Gras celebration.

Members of the Coushatta tribe take part in the National Powwow in Washington, D.C. The Coushatta are one of four federally recognized tribes in Louisiana.

from the Choctaw word *bayuk*, which means "small stream." Another sign of American Indian traditions in Louisiana culture is lagniappe (pronounced LAN-yap). In Louisiana, lagniappe is a little something extra that a shopkeeper or waiter sometimes gives a customer without charging for it. The Spanish picked up the word *yapa* from the Incas of South America, who used the word *yapa* to describe a little bonus given when trading. Many Louisianans believe lagniappe encourages goodwill and friendship.

The Spanish followed the French into Louisiana. Together, the two European groups built a culture that came to be known as Creole, from a Spanish word for people of mixed backgrounds. Wealthy French and Spanish nobles moved to Louisiana and brought European-style art, music, and theater. They built gardens, parks, plantation manors, elegant town-homes, symphony and opera halls, and museums. To be Creole in the early days of the colony meant to be born in Louisiana of only Spanish and French heritage. But as Europeans, American Indians, and African Americans intermarried, being Creole came to mean a person born in Louisiana who had a mixture of French, Spanish, and other backgrounds. Some people still speak a Creole version of French.

Many blacks arrived in Louisiana from West Africa as slaves in the late 1600s and early 1700s. Others came from Caribbean islands as free persons of color. Free people of color were often skilled artisans, such as the blacksmiths who

A band of drummers leads a parade through Congo Square in Louis Armstrong Park in New Orleans.

created the ironwork that adorns buildings throughout the state. Some were highly educated. The Africans who arrived as slaves also brought customs and beliefs from their native cultures. At the time, the area was still under French law, which declared Sundays and religious holidays to be days of rest—even for slaves. On Sundays and holidays, Africans gathered in public and private meeting places. They sold food they had grown and crafts they had made. They practiced West African religious rituals and enjoyed the music, storytelling, and dance of their homelands. Congo Square in present-day Louis Armstrong Park in New Orleans is one such former public gathering place. Many music scholars believe Congo Square was where the musical style known as jazz was first heard.

In the early part of the eighteenth century, German farmers settled along the Mississippi River. French Acadians arrived later in the century, followed by people from the French Caribbean colony

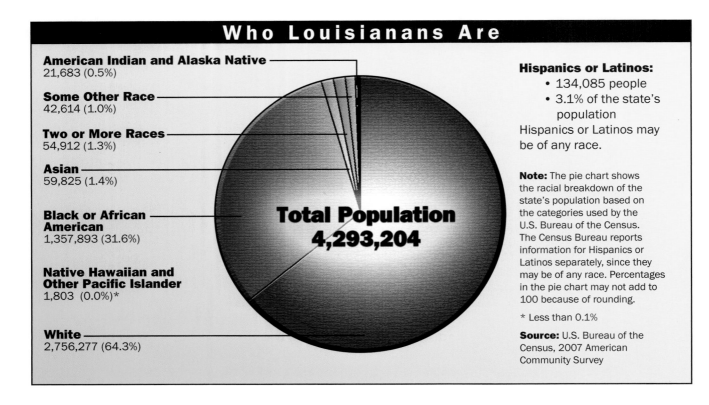

Who Louisianans Are

American Indian and Alaska Native
21,683 (0.5%)

Some Other Race
42,614 (1.0%)

Two or More Races
54,912 (1.3%)

Asian
59,825 (1.4%)

Black or African American
1,357,893 (31.6%)

Native Hawaiian and Other Pacific Islander
1,803 (0.0%)*

White
2,756,277 (64.3%)

Total Population 4,293,204

Hispanics or Latinos:
- 134,085 people
- 3.1% of the state's population

Hispanics or Latinos may be of any race.

Note: The pie chart shows the racial breakdown of the state's population based on the categories used by the U.S. Bureau of the Census. The Census Bureau reports information for Hispanics or Latinos separately, since they may be of any race. Percentages in the pie chart may not add to 100 because of rounding.

* Less than 0.1%

Source: U.S. Bureau of the Census, 2007 American Community Survey

of Saint-Domingue (now the country of Haiti). Spanish-speaking people from the Canary Islands (located between Africa and Spain), called Isleños, settled in St. Bernard and Plaquemines parishes. Irish, English, and Scottish immigrants began arriving from the Appalachian region. At the end of the nineteenth century, Italians, most from Sicily, immigrated to Louisiana, first to farm and later to work in other businesses.

In the twentieth century, immigrants arrived from Latin America and Asia. Louisiana had long had a Hispanic population from the Canary Islands or other former Spanish colonies. But many newer arrivals come from Mexico. The largest Asian population has come from Vietnam. In the 1970s, during and after the Vietnam War, Catholic churches throughout the state sponsored Vietnamese refugees. Many came to Louisiana to start new lives. Some who had fished and shrimped in Asia found the same jobs stateside. In the twenty-first century, the number of Vietnamese immigrants has slowed, but thousands of new residents have come from India, China, and the Philippines.

Life in the North

Louisiana is often separated into north and south. The regions differ in geography and in culture. In northern Louisiana, most residents are of British-American or African-American heritage, though there are smaller groups, such as Czechs, Germans, Italians, and Hungarians. Farming, ranching, and forestry have been traditional ways of life in the region. Natural gas and oil production have become important as well. Large cotton plantations once lined the valuable farmland along the riverbanks known as the "front lands." Away from the main riverbanks, in remote swamps and waterways, people struggled to earn a living in the region called the "back lands," where many still hunt, fish, and trap for income. Today, people who enjoy hunting, boating, and fishing think of the back lands as a special destination.

Set along the Red River, Shreveport is the largest city in northern Louisiana. Shreveport boomed in the 1830s after steamboat captain Henry Shreve cleared the Red River of a logjam that stretched more than 150 miles (240 km). Removing the Great Raft, as the logjam was known, opened up the river to boat traffic. During the Civil War, the city was the capital of Confederate Louisiana. Today, Shreveport is a busy, multicultural center for tourism, commerce, and manufacturing. It has become known as "Hollywood South" for the many movies filmed there.

Farther east is Grambling State University, a historically black college founded in 1901. South of Grambling is a former American Indian trading post, Natchitoches, the oldest settlement in Louisiana. The city of Alexandria, near the geographic center of the state, also is the divide between cultural regions. The area is known as "the crossroads."

Quick Facts

THE BAYOU CLASSIC
The Bayou Classic football game is a Louisiana tradition. Since 1974, the Grambling State Tigers have battled the Jaguars from Baton Rouge's Southern University for bragging rights throughout the state. The battle of the teams' marching bands at halftime is just as popular as the game.

Famous Louisianans

Louis Armstrong: Musician

Born in New Orleans in 1901, Louis Armstrong was one of the greatest jazz musicians who ever lived. His family was poor, and at age thirteen, Armstrong left school and began earning money singing in the streets. He also learned to play the trumpet and the cornet. His talent earned him invitations to play in famous bands. By 1930, he led his own band and performed around the world. Armstrong died in 1971.

Michael DeBakey: Heart Surgeon

Michael DeBakey was born in 1908 in Lake Charles. He developed several devices and techniques for heart surgery and helped establish the National Library of Medicine. He also created the idea of a Mobile Army Surgical Hospital (M.A.S.H.), a movable battlefield hospital that allowed surgeons to quickly operate on injured soldiers. In 1966, he performed the first successful transplant of a partial artificial heart. In 2000, the Library of Congress named him a national "Living Legend."

Mahalia Jackson: Gospel Singer

Mahalia Jackson was born in New Orleans in 1911. Jackson began singing in church at age four. In 1928, she moved to Chicago. While working as a hotel maid, she sang in the Greater Salem Baptist Choir. Soon she was touring and singing in churches and concert halls throughout the country. Before her death in 1972, Jackson had made dozens of influential recordings and performed for audiences around the world.

Ellen DeGeneres: Comedian

Ellen DeGeneres was born in 1958 in Metairie, a suburb of New Orleans. She did not have an easy childhood, but she always kept her sense of humor. Ellen hit the big time in 1984 when she won a televised search for the "Funniest Person in America." Since then, she has starred in two sitcoms and hosted her own talk show. She was chosen as Entertainer of the Year by the magazine *Entertainment Weekly* in 1997. In 2010, DeGeneres became a judge on Fox TV's *American Idol*.

Bobby Jindal: Politician

The son of immigrants, Bobby Jindal was born in Baton Rouge in 1971. Named Piyush by his parents, he called himself Bobby as a child after his TV idol, Bobby Brady of *The Brady Bunch*. He studied biology and public policy in college. Afterward, he combined the two to help Louisiana improve its health department and save money. In 2004, Jindal was elected to the U.S. House of Representatives, only the second Indian American to serve in the lower house of Congress. He became the first Indian-American governor in U.S. history when he was sworn in as governor of Louisiana in January 2008.

Peyton and Eli Manning: Football Players

The Manning family is football royalty in Louisiana. In the 1970s, father Archie Manning starred for the New Orleans Saints of the National Football League (NFL). His sons Peyton (born in 1976) and Eli (born in 1981) were star quarterbacks at Isidore Newman High School in New Orleans. They both went on to greatness in the NFL. Peyton (right) led the Indianapolis Colts to a Super Bowl win in 2007. Eli (left) and the New York Giants won the Super Bowl the following year.

Visitors to New Orleans are never far from music. Here, a crowd gathers to watch a street performance.

Southern Louisiana

Southern Louisiana has very deep French and Catholic roots. Yet the region also has influences from Spain, West Africa, the Caribbean, Mexico, Central America, and many parts of Europe and Asia, as well as from American Indians. One group in particular has fashioned its own unique society. The region of the southwestern prairies and coastal bayous is known as Acadiana, the home of the Cajuns. Though many now work in offices, factories, oil fields, and other businesses, the Cajuns were traditionally fisher folk and farmers with a strong love of music, food, and family life.

African Americans, Germans, and people from Great Britain also migrated to the area. Many of the newcomers adopted the Cajun way of life, including speaking a distinct form of French. Today, Lake Charles is a thriving modern city located in Acadiana. The city of Lafayette, bursting with Cajun restaurants, music clubs, and museums, is one of the cultural centers of the region.

East of Acadiana are the state's largest cities, Baton Rouge and New Orleans. They are also two of the country's largest port cities, with giant docks that are always buzzing with activity and huge storage facilities.

People in New Orleans take great pride in their city and its rich history. The city is known for its historic buildings with decorative ironwork and lush gardens. Nearly all houses have front porches or stoops. Before air-conditioning, many people sat on their porches on hot days to catch any breeze that might blow in from the river.

GUMBO RUN

In many parts of rural Louisiana, gumbo is celebrated in an event called Courir de Mardi Gras, or the Run of Mardi Gras. During the run, riders in costumes gallop on horseback for as many as 60 miles (100 km), stopping along the route to knock on the doors of houses. Once the riders are invited inside, they perform songs and dances until the homeowner gives them an ingredient for making gumbo. When the run ends, riders and their families make a great pot of gumbo that the whole town can enjoy.

A Taste of Louisiana

In northern Louisiana, food is prepared in much the same way it is in other Southern states. In southern Louisiana, there are two popular ways of cooking: Cajun and Creole. Gumbo is one very popular dish in Louisiana. It is also a symbol for the diversity of Louisianans. In the earliest days of the colony, the French prized a European recipe for a tasty seafood soup. In Louisiana, they learned to make do with local ingredients, such as shrimp and crawfish. American Indians added native plants, herbs, and spices to the recipe. The Spanish added hot pepper sauce. African slaves who cooked for the Creole colonists added the vegetable okra. Cajuns contributed tomatoes, turtles, and alligators. Germans added smoked hams and sausages. During Lent (the period between the holy days of Ash Wednesday and Easter), Catholics followed a church rule limiting meat. So vegetables and herbs went into their gumbo recipes. Today, people throughout Louisiana have their own special recipes for gumbo.

A hungry boy enjoys a favorite Louisiana dish, boiled crawfish, during the New Orleans Jazz and Heritage Festival, or JazzFest.

RECIPE FOR PAIN PERDU

Pain perdu is a French phrase meaning "lost bread." Traditional French bread is delicious but quickly dries out. Many Louisiana cooks enjoy making tasty pain perdu using dry French bread.

WHAT YOU NEED

1 orange

3 eggs

$^3/_4$ cup (177 milliliters) milk

$^1/_2$ teaspoon (2.5 grams) cinnamon

$^1/_8$ teaspoon (1 g) nutmeg

2 tablespoon (30 g) granulated sugar

$^1/_2$ teaspoon (2.5 ml) vanilla

$^1/_4$ pound (113 g) butter—1 stick

8 slices day-old French bread (bread must be dry and a little stiff)

Powdered sugar

To prepare the batter, have an adult help you grate the orange rind until you have made about 1 tablespoon (15 g) of zest (grated orange rind). Place the zest in a mixing bowl. Cut the orange and squeeze the juice into a measuring cup. Take 1/4 cup (60 ml) of the juice and add it to the zest in the bowl. Add eggs, milk, spices, granulated sugar, and vanilla. Stir with a fork or whisk until the sugar dissolves.

Have an adult help you use the stove. Heat 2 tablespoons (30 g) of the butter in a frying pan on medium-high heat.

Dip two slices of bread into the egg-milk mixture. Allow extra liquid to drain back into the mixing bowl. Place the slices of bread into the frying pan. Cook until the slices are golden brown, about 2–3 minutes. Using a spatula, flip the bread and allow the other side to cook. Repeat for the rest of the slices. Sprinkle with powdered sugar and serve warm.

Les Bon Temps (The Good Times)

From farmers' fields, city streets, and backwater bayous to church halls, riverboats, and clubs, the special music of Louisiana rings out. American music forms such as Western swing, blues, and gospel are heard throughout Louisiana.

When Cajuns first came to Louisiana, they brought Acadian fiddle music. After German farmers moved to Acadiana, they introduced the accordion to their Cajun neighbors. Since then, the accordion has been the soul of Cajun music. African Americans added washboard strumming and other rhythms to the Cajun sound to create the lively dance music called zydeco. New Orleans has long been famous for jazz music. Early stars were Louis Armstrong and Jelly Roll Morton. Louisiana

A zydeco band performs at New Orleans JazzFest.

Mardi Gras parades feature elaborate, colorful floats. Here, parade-goers cheer a float that honors the crawfish.

musicians Fats Domino and Jerry Lee Lewis were early rock 'n' roll stars. Today, New Orleans is one of the world's best cities for listening to jazz, blues, rock, gospel, Cajun, zydeco, hip-hop, and more.

Louisiana is rich in festivals. The French expression *Laissez les bon temps rouler*, which means "Let the good times roll," is often heard in Louisiana. There

are many music festivals. The love of food is revealed in festivals devoted entirely to gumbo, jambalaya, oysters, pralines, meat pies, shrimp, catfish, crawfish, strawberries, and other foods. The ethnic heritage of the state is honored in festivals such as Czech Days, German Oktoberfest, Laotian New Year, Calling of the Tribes Powwow, and Isleños Festival.

Festivals celebrating religious holidays are also very important to Louisiana residents. In December, communities throughout the state celebrate the holiday season with a Festival of Lights. Mardi Gras, which in English means "Fat Tuesday," is a traditional Roman Catholic carnival that takes place just before Lent begins. Lent is a forty-day period between Ash Wednesday and Easter. According to the Christian faith, followers should deny themselves too much food, drink, and merriment during Lent. So Mardi Gras symbolizes the last chance until Easter for a lot of food, music, and fun.

There are Mardi Gras celebrations throughout the state, but one of the biggest in the world is in New Orleans. In that city, Mardi Gras is an official holiday. Citizens decorate the city in the official colors of gold, purple, and green. There are masked balls and parades for weeks leading up to Mardi Gras. People dressed in colorful feathers, beads, and glitter ride elaborate floats. On Mardi Gras, more than a millions parade-goers line the streets and reach out to capture beads, festival coins, and other holiday trinkets thrown from the floats.

Louisiana's unique blend of ethnic and religious traditions has always helped it stand apart from other states. Citizens are proud of their culture.

MAKING A MARDI GRAS MASK

People celebrate Mardi Gras by dressing in colorful costumes and masks. Follow these instructions to make your own Mardi Gras mask.

WHAT YOU NEED

Newspaper

A pencil

A piece of cardboard—about 8 inches (20 cm) by 11 inches (28 cm)

Scissors

Tacky glue

Artificial feathers (sold in craft stores or toy departments) or sheets of colored tissue paper

1-yard (0.9-m) strand of sequin or shiny ribbon

1 yard (0.9 m) of colored ribbon (found in craft or fabric stores)

A large wooden chopstick or a new, unsharpened pencil

Packing tape or other strong tape

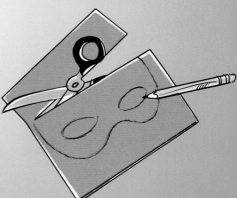

Spread newspaper on your worktable and set up all your supplies. Draw a half-mask shape on the cardboard. A half-mask would cover your face from your forehead to your nose. Make sure the mask is wide enough to fit the width of your face. Cut out two large oval-shaped eyeholes. If the cardboard is hard to cut, ask an adult to help you.

Drop a small amount of glue along the upper edge of the mask. Set the feathers so that the stems are glued to the mask, and the feathery tips point outward. Continue gluing feathers around the mask.

Once done, layer the rest of the feathers over the remaining blank space on the mask. Use scissors to trim the feathers as needed. (If you cannot find feathers, use sheets of different colored tissue paper, cut into small pieces.)

Cut the strand of shiny ribbon into three sections. Two pieces should be long enough to fit around the eyeholes. The third piece should fit along the edge of the entire mask. Glue the ribbon around each eyehole and then around the outside edge of the mask. Use scissors to trim any excess ribbon. Allow the glue to dry before proceeding to the next step.

Place a few drops of glue around the sides of the stick and at the top and bottom. Tightly wrap the colored ribbon around the stick from top to bottom. Let the glue dry before attaching the stick to the mask.

Using small pieces of tape, attach the top of the stick to one side of the mask, away from the eyehole. Now, you are ready for Mardi Gras. Let the good times roll!

Calendar of Events

★ Sugar Bowl

Each January, the Louisiana Superdome hosts one of college football's oldest bowl games. Two of the top teams in the country have met in the Sugar Bowl every year since 1934.

★ Calling of the Tribes Powwow

Hosted by the Houma tribe in Grand Bois Park, this three-day celebration in March includes tribal dancing competitions, drumming, American Indian arts and crafts, and tasty foods such as fry bread and shrimp patties.

★ New Orleans Jazz and Heritage Festival

In spring, people from around the world visit New Orleans to hear some of the top acts in jazz and other styles of music. They also come to admire traditional and contemporary crafts, including decorative gourds and paintings, and to enjoy African, Cajun, Creole, Latino, and American Indian food and culture.

★ Isleños Festival

In March in St. Bernard Parish, descendants of the Isleños people of the Canary Islands celebrate two centuries in Louisiana with food, folklore exhibits, music, arts and crafts, cooking competitions, and games.

★ Festival International de Louisiane

The last week of April turns downtown Lafayette into a giant stage. Performers from such faraway places as Senegal, Brazil, Congo, and Quebec join popular Louisiana Cajun and zydeco musicians for a five-day celebration of music, food, art, and dance.

★ Mudbug Madness

On Memorial Day weekend, the people of Shreveport celebrate one of Louisiana's favorite activities—the crawfish boil. More than 60,000 pounds (27,200 kg) of crawfish are cooked while thousands of people pour into town to enter crawfish-eating contests, watch clowns and jugglers, and listen to music.

★ Frog Fest

In August, the town of Rayne polishes the frog murals on its buildings and celebrates the common Louisiana swamp dweller. Festivities include a Frog Festival Queen's ball and the International Frog Racing and Jumping Contest.

★ Louisiana Sugar Cane Festival

Every September, in Iberia Parish, Louisianans celebrate their Cajun heritage with parades, fireworks, a *fais do-do* dance party, the crowning of the Sugar Queen, and other sweet festivities.

★ Swamp Fest at the Audubon Zoo

Thousands visit the Audubon Zoo in New Orleans in October to feed animals in the swamp exhibit, taste fried alligator and catfish po'boy sandwiches, and listen to Cajun and zydeco music.

★ La Toussaint

November 1, the day after Halloween, is All Saints' Day, a Catholic holiday that honors Christian saints. Louisianans call it La Toussaint. Every year, people across the state continue a tradition started by colonists— cleaning tombs and leaving flowers at graveyards.

★ Festival of Lights

Natchitoches holds a Christmas celebration on the first Saturday in December. At the end of a fun-filled day, 300,000 colored lights strung through the town and along the nearby lake are switched on until New Year's Day.

How the Government Works

There are three levels of government in Louisiana: city or town, parish, and state. In individual cities and towns, people elect mayors or council members to run the local government. Local government units made up of various towns and cities are called parishes in Louisiana. Most other states call these units counties. Louisiana's original Catholic parishes started under Spanish and French rule. In 1807, these boundaries were used to help mark regional governments. Voters in forty-one of the state's sixty-four parishes elect a group called a police jury to manage their government. A few parishes have a commission and elect commissioners to run the government.

At the level of state government, voters elect senators and representatives to the state legislature, judges, a governor, and other executive office holders. Like citizens in all other states, Louisianans also elect people to

In Their Own Words

Baton Rouge was clothed in flowers, like a bride—no, much more so; like a greenhouse. . . . The magnolia-trees in the Capitol grounds were lovely and fragrant, with their dense rich foliage and huge snow-ball blossoms. The scent of the flower is very sweet, but you want distance on it, because it is so powerful.

—Mark Twain, in his book
Life on the Mississippi

The Louisiana State Capitol in Baton Rouge is the tallest capitol in the United States. It stands 450 feet (137 m) tall.

Branches of Government

EXECUTIVE ★ ★ ★ ★ ★ ★ ★ ★

The governor is the head of the executive branch. The people of Louisiana choose a governor every four years. He or she can serve only two terms in a row. The governor appoints cabinet members and signs bills into law. Other executive branch offices include the lieutenant governor, attorney general, treasurer, and superintendent of education.

LEGISLATIVE ★ ★ ★ ★ ★ ★ ★ ★

The legislative branch is made up of the state senate, with 39 members, and the state house of representatives, with 105 members. State legislators are elected for four-year terms and cannot be elected more than twice in a row. They meet each year for up to sixty working days. When not working at the Capitol in Baton Rouge, legislators meet with people in the area they represent. Often they hold other jobs, too, working as farmers, business owners, pharmacists, and lawyers.

JUDICIAL ★ ★ ★ ★ ★ ★ ★ ★

The judicial branch is a system of courts made up of the state supreme court, courts of appeal, and district courts. Most trials are decided by district courts. These courts hear criminal cases and settle arguments over laws. The next level is the court of appeals. If someone does not believe he or she received a fair ruling in the district courts, court of appeals judges will hear the reasons and rule on whether to uphold or overturn the district court decision. Some cases are appealed from a court of appeals to the state supreme court for final ruling. The supreme court has a chief justice and six associate justices who are each elected from a separate district. Judges in the appeals and supreme courts serve ten-year terms.

represent them in the U.S. Congress in Washington, D.C. As of 2010, Louisiana had seven representatives in the U.S. House of Representatives. Voters elect one representative for their district every two years. Voters statewide elect two U.S. senators, who serve six-year terms.

How a Bill Becomes a Law

State senators and representatives, who together are called legislators, create and pass laws. A law can be started in either the state house of representatives or the state senate. To begin, a legislator proposes an idea for a law. Sometimes these ideas come from the state residents whom the legislator represents.

The idea is clearly spelled out in a document called a bill. The legislator who proposes it becomes the bill's sponsor. For example, in 2009, Louisiana Representative Nickie Monica wanted to encourage safety in motor vehicles. He proposed a bill that would fine people for not wearing seatbelts. "We know it's going to save lives," he said.

A clerk drafted Representative Monica's bill and assigned the bill a number (HB 499). Next the bill was read aloud in the house. Then the bill was assigned to a committee to discuss it. During committee meetings, members review bills and listen to people who have come to talk about why they are in favor of or oppose a certain bill. After the meetings, the committee decides whether to approve the bill. If the committee approves the bill, it is then read out loud again. A bill must be read in each chamber on at least three separate occasions. At this time, all the

Louisiana governor Bobby Jindal prepares to sign a bill into law.

Contacting Lawmakers

★ ★ ★ ★ ★ ★ ★ ★ ★ ★ ★ ★

Citizens can share their thoughts on an issue with any of Louisiana's state legislators. Go to

http://legis.state.la.us

Scroll down the page and look under "Your Louisiana Legislators." The linked page will help citizens find the legislators who represent the area in which they live.

representatives can debate the bill and suggest changes. Each time a bill is changed, or amended, the representatives vote.

Once the bill passed the house, it moved to the senate. There, it was reviewed by another committee. Once approved by the committee, the bill was amended and voted on. If the senate passes a bill but makes amendments, the bill must be returned to the house for review before being presented to the governor. If the house approves the changes, it delivers the bill to the governor for signature. If the governor signs the bill, it becomes law. Governor Bobby Jindal signed Representative Monica's bill, which became a law known as Act 166 of 2009.

However, the governor may veto, or refuse to sign, a bill. A vetoed bill is sent back to the legislature. There, lawmakers decide whether to let the bill fail or to override the governor's veto and pass the law. To override a veto, both houses must vote in favor of the bill by a two-thirds majority.

Speaking Up

Louisianans have always known the power of the people. Louisiana's citizens and lawmakers know that everyone's voice is important, no matter how rich or poor, how old or young. Citizens throughout the state's long history have fought for fair and equal rights.

For example, in 1960, a Louisiana first grader and her family spoke out against racial inequality in schools. Ruby Bridges was a young African-American girl who had moved to New Orleans with her family. The federal government in Washington, D.C., had ordered New Orleans to desegregate its schools. Black students could no longer be kept out of white schools. This angered many white

Federal marshals escort six-year-old Ruby Bridges to school. She needed protection from protesters who did not want her to attend a white school.

people in the city. On November 14, 1960, six-year-old Ruby Bridges walked beside four federal marshals through an angry crowd of white protesters to enter an all-white elementary school. When Ruby returned to school the next day, she walked into an empty classroom. All the white families had taken their children out of school. Each day after that, Ruby's teacher taught her only student. And each day, Ruby walked past protesters yelling and throwing things at her on the way to school. A year later, the school was fully integrated. Ruby was no longer the only black student in the building, and white and black students attended the school together.

Few children are expected to act as bravely as Ruby Bridges, but all students should speak up for what they believe in. Desegregation in Louisiana—and in the rest of the country—occurred because people fought for what they believed was right. They voiced their opinions and influenced legislators to create laws for equality. This still holds true today. Each year, Louisiana state legislators visit hundreds of public schools and tell the students, "Your ideas count!"

Making a Living

Louisianans have lived through difficult cycles of economic gain and loss. For example, many people lost their livelihood as a result of Hurricane Katrina in 2005. But from 2005 to 2008, the average Louisianan's income increased by nearly half. Most of the increase was the result of financial aid from the U.S. government. State leaders also took steps to improve conditions for citizens. Louisiana fared better than most states when economic troubles caused millions of people nationwide to lose their jobs in 2008 and 2009. There are many reasons why a greater percentage of people born in Louisiana choose to stay in their home state than natives of any other state.

Agriculture

Louisiana is blessed with rich soil and a climate that is ideal for growing a variety of crops. The major crops are cotton, sugar, rice, corn, and soybeans. There are more than 8 million acres (3.2 million hectares) of farmland in the state. Louisiana's crops are sold throughout the country.

Rice is an important crop to Louisiana farmers. African slaves first brought rice seed to the Louisiana prairies as early as 1718. Rice grew well in the wet soil, but it did not become popular until after the Civil War. In the 1800s, Cajun and German rice farmers used floodwaters from the Mississippi River to grow rice. Residents later developed irrigation channels to provide the water for the

Children in St. Tammany Parish enjoy fishing in Lake Pontchartrain. Fishing is also big business in Louisiana.

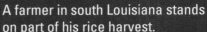
A farmer in south Louisiana stands on part of his rice harvest.

crop. In the 1950s, rice farmers added crawfish to their flooded fields. After the farmers harvested the rice, the crawfish would eat algae and rotting plant matter. The crawfish could later be harvested for food, providing a second crop. In addition to providing crops, the crawfish–rice fields have become important wetlands for wildlife.

More than a quarter of Louisiana is covered by farms. A third of that land is used for pasture and livestock. Grass grows year-round in the warm, wet climate, so cattle have plenty of fresh grazing land. Farmers also raise hogs and goats. But despite the variety of crops and livestock, fewer people have jobs in farming each year. Large corporations and successful landowners now operate about half of the state's farmland. These large farms earn greater profits and can afford expensive farm machinery. The machines are extremely efficient and do much of the work once done by farm laborers.

Fishing

More than a billion pounds of fish and shellfish are harvested in the state each year. Louisiana's commercial fishers catch about 10 percent of all seafood in the United States. The state produces more shrimp and oysters than any other state. Other prized seafood includes crab, red snapper, and yellowfin tuna. Freshwater fishers catch crawfish and catfish. But these creatures are also raised in fish farms.

Louisiana has tens of thousands of jobs in the fishing industry. Besides being fishers, people work at selling, shipping, processing, and packaging fish. Thousands of others build and maintain boats, gear, and supplies for the fishing industry.

A worker unloads shrimp from a shrimp boat in the small coastal town of Empire, Louisiana.

Workers & Industries

Industry	Number of People Working in That Industry	Percentage of All Workers Who Are Working in That Industry
Education and health care	410,884	21.7%
Wholesale and retail businesses	285,325	15.1%
Publishing, media, entertainment, hotels, and restaurants	206,106	10.9%
Construction	175,443	9.3%
Manufacturing	164,312	8.7%
Professionals, scientists, and managers	157,304	8.3%
Transportation and public utilities	104,571	5.5%
Banking and finance, insurance, and real estate	103,767	5.5%
Other services	101,522	5.4%
Government	98,058	5.2%
Farming, fishing, forestry, and mining	85,104	4.5%
Totals	1,892,396	100%

Notes: Figures above do not include people in the armed forces. "Professionals" includes people such as doctors and lawyers. Percentages may not add to 100 because of rounding.

Source: U.S. Bureau of the Census, 2007 estimates

Forestry and Wood Products

More than half of Louisiana is covered by forests. Pine, oak, sweetgum, cypress, and other trees are harvested. About 15,000 people have jobs cutting, transporting, or processing timber. Wood in Louisiana is used to make paper, boxes, shopping bags, furniture, and construction materials, as well as baseball bats, musical instruments, and boats. Each year, the forest and forest products industries add about $3 billion to the economy of the state.

Natural Gas, Oil, Mining, and Manufacturing

In the 1870s, companies drilled wells in search of water to make ice. One evening, a night watchman at an ice factory in Shreveport felt wind coming from a well that was being drilled. When he lit a match to investigate, he caused an explosion. Natural gas, not water, had been flowing through the pipe. Gas from the well was soon piped to the factory to provide energy for lighting. This was the beginning of Louisiana's oil and natural gas industry.

The first successful oil well in Louisiana was drilled in 1901 near the town of Jennings, a farming community halfway between Lafayette and Lake Charles. Since that time, rice farmers and swamp fishers along the coast have lived and worked side by side with oil field workers. After World War II, major oil fields were discovered in the Gulf of Mexico. In 1947, the first drilling platforms were built offshore out of sight of land. Today, Louisiana is the nation's fourth-largest producer of oil.

But the state does not just drill the oil. Louisiana's ports also bring in a fifth of the foreign oil used by Americans. The state is a very important storage center for oil and natural gas. Massive salt caves have been filled with oil for emergencies. Dozens of pipelines deliver oil and natural gas from Louisiana to states as far away as Wisconsin.

Louisiana's mines provide important minerals such as sulfur and salt. Louisiana has huge underground rock salt formations. Some are 50,000 feet (15,240 m) deep and stretch for a mile across. In 1862, the nation's first rock salt mine was dug on Avery Island. Salt is commonly used for cooking, but it

This oil rig is one of hundreds found in the Gulf of Mexico.

also has uses in paper-making, soap-making, fabric dyeing, and other areas of manufacturing. Around the country, millions of pounds of rock salt are used each winter to de-ice roads and make them safe for driving.

The Louisiana Gulf Coast is key to the nation's petrochemical industry. Petrochemical refineries are factories that turn crude oil and natural gas liquids into plastics, fertilizers, synthetic (human-made) rubber, and other products. Louisiana's oil refineries produce more than 15 billion gallons (56 billion liters) of gasoline each year. The refineries also produce jet fuel. Large aerospace companies have factories in the area. Michoud Assembly Facility in New Orleans was used to build rockets for trips to the moon.

People in the state also make well-drilling platforms, ships of all sizes, small trucks, telephones, glass, marine radar, clothing, and hundreds of other products.

Transportation

Steamboats began traveling the Mississippi River in 1811, carrying cargo to and from New Orleans and the rest of the world. Louisiana has the nation's second-largest number of navigable waterways. Today, there are more than thirty ports in the state. The Port of South Louisiana is the nation's largest by tonnage carried. It spans the area between New Orleans and Baton Rouge. Nearby, the Port of New Orleans handles more dry bulk cargo than any other port in the country. Dry bulk products such as corn from the Midwest can be poured into large holds in a ship and sucked out at their destination. Deepwater docks at these ports have nearby storage facilities for foods such as tropical fruits and coffee beans. Dock areas also have grain silos, oil tanks, and steel yards and lumberyards. Using natural rivers and lakes and human-made channels, Louisiana has created an intracoastal waterway. It allows ocean freighters to travel the entire coastline, safe from storms in the Gulf of Mexico. About one in seven jobs in the state depends on its waterways. The ports at Baton Rouge and Lake Charles are also huge contributors to the state's economy.

Service Industries

The service industry is the biggest job sector in the state. People who hold service jobs may work in schools, stores, warehouses, banks, hospitals, museums, restaurants, hotels, or other businesses.

Tourism is a leading industry in the state. Visitors from around the nation and the world come to Louisiana. Some come to hunt and fish in Louisiana's rivers, lakes, and wetlands. Nature lovers can camp, hike, and bird-watch in Louisiana's twenty state parks. Other visitors take a cultural journey to view the grand nineteenth-century plantation houses along the River Road or to sample the unique food and music of Acadiana.

Products & Resources

Tabasco Sauce

After the Civil War, Edmund McIlhenny returned to his sugar plantation and salt mine on Avery Island to find nearly everything destroyed. But the special hot Mexican peppers he had planted before the war had survived. He used the peppers to create a popular hot sauce called Tabasco. Today, the McIlhenny family's company sells millions of bottles of the spicy sauce each year.

Shrimp

Louisiana is a longtime leader in America's shrimp harvest. Brown and white shrimp are the most popular. Brown shrimp are most abundant in late spring and early summer. White shrimp are harvested in late summer and early fall.

Fertilizer

Special manufacturing plants in Louisiana produce ammonia from the hydrogen in natural gas. Much of the ammonia is used in the fertilizers that help plants grow. The Baton Rouge area makes about a quarter of America's ammonia.

Sugarcane

Sugarcane has been grown in Louisiana since the 1700s. Priests from Europe first brought the crop and sold the stalks to be chewed. In 1796, Etienne de Boré became the first Louisianan to sell his granulated sugar to other states. Today, sugarcane fields in Louisiana yield 30 to 50 tons (27 to 45 metric tons) of sugarcane per acre. From each ton, 175 to 225 pounds (79 to 102 kg) of sugar is produced.

Oil

Supertankers, each of which can carry 4 million barrels of crude oil from overseas, need very deep water to dock and a lot of room to move around. Only one port in the country has waters deep enough to unload oil from these giant tankers—the Louisiana Offshore Oil Port. The "superport" was completed in 1981. The oil is pumped from the tankers and sent to shore by underwater pipelines.

Tourism

Travelers visiting Louisiana once spent more than $10 billion a year in the state. The effects of Hurricane Katrina lowered tourism income in the years after 2005, but only so many visitors can stay away. The French Quarter of New Orleans, historic countryside plantations, and the music of Acadiana are just some of the attractions that still draw millions of visitors every year.

Destination: New Orleans

A large portion of tourism in Louisiana is centered in New Orleans. The "Big Easy" is full of world-famous theaters, museums, restaurants, and music clubs. Football fans flock to the Superdome to cheer for the New Orleans Saints. The team gained countless new fans after winning its first Super Bowl in February 2010. Basketball fans head to the New Orleans Arena to watch the New Orleans Hornets. Visitors spend more than $4 billion in the city each year. One-fourth of that is spent during the famous Mardi Gras celebration.

Many people visit Louisiana to see its amazing architecture. Each year, people come to admire buildings designed in European and Caribbean styles in New Orleans. Throughout the state, visitors can see historic buildings, traditional plantations, and other sites that serve as reminders of the state's past.

Quarterback Drew Brees raises the championship trophy after the New Orleans Saints' victory in Super Bowl XLIV.

Jackson Square is a favorite tourist spot in New Orleans. St. Louis Cathedral, seen in the background, and the surrounding buildings were constructed in the 1700s.

Ecotourism

A newer addition to the tourist industry is ecotourism. Ecotourism is travel based on viewing nature and wildlife, such as bird-watching or taking a swamp tour. Several wilderness swamps are within an hour's drive of New Orleans, which was itself built on drained swampland. People travel by boat into Louisiana's swamps. They navigate around cypress trees dripping with Spanish moss to see alligators, water moccasins, egrets, eagles, and other wild creatures in their natural habitats.

But Louisiana's swamps and coastal wetlands have been seriously suffering. Each year, about 24 square miles (62 sq km) of coastal wetlands are washed away. That equals the loss of land area the size of a football field

A boy examines water hyacinth, a nonnative plant that is causing trouble in Louisiana waterways. Learning about such threats helps Louisianans protect their environment.

every forty-five minutes. In the past, the Mississippi River naturally changed directions, bringing soil from lands farther upriver to create "new land" in the delta. But thousands of human-made levees, dams, and channels along the Mississippi and the rivers that feed into it have directed the water away from its natural course. New wetlands are not being naturally created to make up for the land lost each year. The wetlands protect wildlife, but they also protect the coastline from the Gulf of Mexico's violent storms. As Hurricane Katrina showed, the homes, businesses, docks, and fuel pipelines of southern Louisiana are in danger of being washed away.

The enormous burden of maintaining and protecting the wetlands is more than the state can handle alone. Louisiana's leaders want the federal government to provide more help. They want states farther north along the Mississippi to contribute, too. Louisiana's seafood harvest is shipped around the nation. Most of the continent's migratory birds stop over in the Pelican State. The problems of coastal Louisiana are the problems of the entire United States. Ecotours into these unique regions teach visitors what every resident already knows: Louisiana is a special place.

State Flag & Seal

The people of Louisiana kept true to its nickname, the Pelican State, by adopting this flag in 1912. A white-and-gold pelican feeds its young, centered on a solid blue background. Underneath the pelicans' nest is a white ribbon that bears the state motto: "Union, Justice and Confidence."

The official state seal looks a lot like the flag. It was adopted in 1902. Inside the circle is a brown pelican in a nest with three of her young. The mother pelican is picking at her chest to feed her young rather than letting them starve.

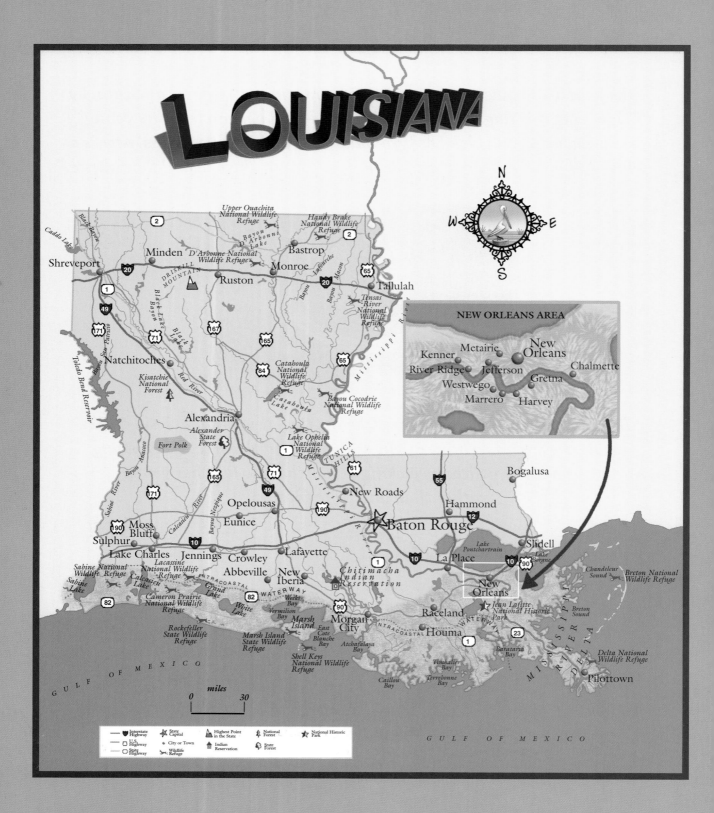

LOUISIANA

NEW ORLEANS AREA

Kenner · Metairie · New Orleans
River Ridge · Jefferson · Chalmette
Westwego · Gretna
Marrero · Harvey

Minden · Bastrop · Monroe
Shreveport · Ruston · Tallulah

Natchitoches

Alexandria

Opelousas
Eunice
Moss Bluff
Sulphur · Lake Charles · Jennings · Crowley · Lafayette
Abbeville · New Iberia · Morgan City
Raceland · Houma

New Roads · Baton Rouge
Bogalusa
Hammond
La Place · Slidell
New Orleans
Pilottown

State Song

Give Me Louisiana

words and music by Doralice Fontane

Give me Loui - si - an - a, The State where I was born, The State of snow - y cot - ton, The best I've ev - er known; A State of sweet mag - no - lias, And cre - ole mel - o - dies. Oh give me Loui - si - an - a, The State where I was born. Oh what sweet old mem - 'ries The mos - sy old oaks bring! It brings us the sto - ry of our E - van - ge - line. A State of old tra - di - tion, of old plan - ta - tion days Makes good old Loui - si - an - a The sweet - est of all States.

Louisiana has two official state songs. "Give Me Louisiana" was adopted in 1970.
The popular sing-along "You Are My Sunshine" was adopted as the second state song in 1977.

BOOKS

Bernard, Shane K. *Cajuns and Their Acadian Ancestors: A Young Reader's History*. Jackson, MS: University Press of Mississippi, 2008.

Bridges, Ruby. *Through My Eyes/Ruby Bridges: Articles and Interviews*. New York: Scholastic Press, 1999.

McNeese, Tim. *Plessy v. Ferguson: Separate but Equal*. New York: Chelsea House, 2006.

Miller, Debra. *Hurricane Katrina: Devastation on the Gulf Coast*. Detroit: Lucent Books, 2006.

Shea, Therese. *The Louisiana Purchase*. New York: PowerKids Press, 2009.

Worth, Richard. *Louisiana, 1682–1803*. Washington, DC: National Geographic Society, 2005.

WEBSITES

Louisiana Department of Culture, Recreation, and Tourism:
http://www.crt.state.la.us

Louisiana House of Representatives Kids' Page:
http://house.legis.state.la.us/pubinfo/Kids.htm

The Official State of Louisiana Kids' Page:
http://www.louisiana.gov/Explore/Kids_Page

Ruth Bjorklund lives on Bainbridge Island, across Puget Sound from Seattle, Washington, with her husband, two children, and many pets. Ruth has written several nonfiction books for students on a variety of topics. She has visited every state in the country, and Louisiana is definitely a favorite.

Andy Steinitz has written and edited educational and reference materials for *The World Almanac*, Borders Books, and *The New York Times*. He thanks his many Cajun friends who fed him gumbo and crawfish for inspiration. Steinitz currently works at Pratt Institute. He lives in Brooklyn, NY.

Page numbers in **boldface** are illustrations.